a collection of love, loss and longing

Printed in Great Britain
First paperback edition: February 2021
ISBN: 979-8567143308

Writer: Sai Assari
Cover Designer and Illustrator: Nadia Hussain
Digital Artist: Samiha Yasmin Chowdhury

Contact: saiassai1998@gmail.com

To a Lord Who listens
& to the dreams
that He answers

Preface

I've always believed dreams were the mind's way of compensating for things absent in our lives. During the toughest times, I have dreams where I'm finally at ease. Where I'm certain that I'll never experience another hardship again.

If I miss my late grandmother, she shows up in my dreams. The same silver hair and that toothless grin.

Outside my dreams, I remember my anxieties. The Uyghur Muslims in China; the covid-19 pandemic. Human corruption, which is as native to this world as the trees and its oceans.

Sleep, sometimes, serves as the only relief.

There's this belief in Islam, when during those hours we're asleep, our soul is taken to *Barzakh*, a realm beyond space and time. Perhaps this is why when we dream, our minds, too, take us to an alternate reality. Sometimes, the dreams that the mind conjures are euphoric, other times, they reflect our deepest fears.

This leads me to the title of this book.

Dreams. A collection of dreams. I want to focus on that point when you awaken from a deep slumber, but want to fall back into bed, because reality doesn't compare to the imagination.

So, here's a compilation of prose and poetry that I hope will enrich your noons, give colour to your nights, and make you feel like you're wide-awake in the realms of *Barzakh*.

Happy reading,
and sweet dreams.

Sai

sai assari

Isra & Khalid

In which 41 excerpts are used
to tell the story of two individuals
and their life together.

❄ 01 – Rainfall

Tonight the rain falls in heaps, and Isra's brother finds her leaning against her bedroom window, nursing a warm cup of chai between her hands. He's smirking, like he has secrets to tell and he's desperate to let them spill from his lips.

He tells her their father has found her the perfect match, if she's interested.

"You'll like him." Her brother assures her. "I met him last *jummah*. He's a good guy, Khalid. A fitness instructor."

"No I -" Isra hesitates. "I'm not interested." She turns her back to him, shoulders stiffening, and her mind wanders back to suppressed memories from childhood: Waking to the sound of her mother's downpour, her father's explosive thunder. She thinks about a long messy divorce and two children that had suffered because of it.

"Marriage…you know the idea of it scares me," she finally admits.

And her brother sighs. He says, "how come?"

He says, "maybe marriage isn't what scares you, Isra."

He says,

"maybe it's marrying the wrong person that does."

❄ 02 – Sunset

He's been trying to act all chill around her but he's so uncool he thinks it's causing climate change. He's been up since 3:12 this morning googling "how do I make her happy" until he realised that just...wasn't normal. He's reading about cosmos because he's heard she's fascinated by the stars. He's chewing on his thumb and taking notes about picnics. He's mentally drawing up lists of interesting conversation starters but he knows his throat is going to dry up when she looks at him.

He's never seen her smile but he can imagine it. He can't stop thinking about her, talking about her.

"My sister Isra, you kinda like her, huh?" Her brother beams.

Yeah. Kinda. A little.

It's just when she's around the world dresses up in better colours and he can't envision himself coming home to anyone else.

He drops his face into his hands. Sighs.

Yeah. Kinda.

Just a little.

❄ 03 – Fireworks

It smells like spring in the morning. Isra's father finds her in the kitchen and sits her down.

"What do you think of the young man?"

Isra drops her plate in the sink. Tries to ignore the blush creeping up her neck at the mention of Khalid.

She sighs a breath. "I like him."

Her father smiles. And it looks like fireworks. Exploding.

Big and bright and ecstatic.

❄ 04 – Forever

"Say something."
The world is white noise. Right now
she can't comprehend the colour of the sky.
    "I-I don't know what to say-"
He slips the ring onto her finger.
    "Say yes."

❈ 05 – Their life will be like this

In the warm afternoon they roast their vegetables. Their home is on the edge of all things. And in the quiet you might hear the ocean. Maybe they'll invite their families or friends. Or maybe they'll eat alone. He'll cut her some fruit; she'll pour him honeyed water. Maybe they'll eat outside. He'll tease her like he always does. She'll pretend to be mad about it. And once their bellies are full, they'll blow the sun out like a matchstick, and the sky will darken into a soft bruise. It's so easy to fall asleep, curled up against each other, forgotten, by the world.

❄ 06 – Because he is

She felt like she'd always known him on some soul level. Like she'd been searching for his face since the beginning of her life. Like long ago a string was wrapped around his finger connected to hers, and he's been tugging her towards him since.

He saw her when she was scared and lonely and thought, "I want to learn you," and he did.

He pressed his palms against the walls of her heart and mumbled, "I know you don't trust
so I'll earn it."

He sat himself on the dirty grounds beside her and said, "I know you're hurt.
I'll give you time to heal."

If she hasn't washed her hair in days, he'll still run his fingers through it. She thinks he might have blinders on and can't see all her flaws and cracks and tape that's barely holding her together. But somehow, he'll still hold her, laugh at her clumsiness and tuck her in at 2 AM after she's shattered something and he's left to mop the floors and sweep up the pieces she couldn't pick up herself.

She doesn't know why he's staying. But it doesn't matter.

Because he is.

❋ 07 – Garments

"Why are you so good to me?"

Khalid rips off the underlayer of the plaster with his teeth.

He wraps it, carefully, around the gash on her finger. Brings the plastered wound to his lips. Kisses it. 'You're my wife."

And he leaves it as that. So simply. Like it's the only answer that could ever make sense.

~

Men seem to want women with vulnerability. Something delicate they can protect from the wind. But that's not it for him.

It's just nice knowing someone else gets scared of things, you know? It's nice to feel like you're needed. Like the sky isn't the sky without you.

His grandmother tells him marriage is both giving and taking. You're garments for each other. She'll be your comfort and you'll be her shelter. It's a two-way street and you meet in the middle.

Always. Forever.

❄ 08 – Sleep

"I'm a man, not a pillow. Stop cuddling me."

"But you're so warm."

Khalid tries to pry her off. It has absolutely no effect whatsoever. He sighs, wrapping one arm around her.

It's not that he has a problem with being cuddled. Cuddling's nice, as a concept. It's just that his wife doesn't know *how* to. She wraps her arms and legs around him like he's her opponent in a wrestling arena, and she's about to knock him out cold with her signature and most deadly move.

He'd get used to it, eventually. Probably.

"Khalid?" Isra murmurs. Her breath is hot against his neck. He presses her closer.

"Hmm?"

"Will you always stay with me?"

He smiles at that. "Yes."

"Until we're very old?"

"Very old."

"For always?"

"Yeah, for always.

Now *go to sleep.*"

❄ 09 – Abandoned city

He used to feel like an abandoned city but when she came, every streetlight in him awakened. Like she filled the corners of him with glow sticks. He hasn't been with her for long, but he's already forgotten how he survived without her. Doesn't know how he fell in love. Just that he woke up one morning in the centre of it. Or it probably hit him last weekend when she went to visit her parents and stayed the week. It took everything in him to stop himself from reaching for his car keys, for his phone - every minute.

Scary, isn't it? When your whole existence feels like it's defined by another person. When the empty chair beside him taunts him. When she's the only person he wants to talk to about how hard it is not being able to talk to her.

He's got a million thoughts and fears and things going on. But then he's pressing the doorbell of her childhood house and everything dark disintegrates at the sight of her face when she opens the door.

Man, it's the smallest things that do him in. Sometimes in the dark when they're watching movies, he senses her turn, just a little, to see if he's enjoying what's going on. Her humming in the kitchen. Her questionable cooking. Her clumsy feet.

The smallness of her. How she can only manage to grip four of his fingers when she's holding his hands.

"What's one thing you can't stand about me?" she asks him in the car when he's driving her home.

Your absence. He wants to answer. *All the empty space you leave behind.*

"You're the messiest person I've ever met," he says instead, turning the corner. "It's infuriating."

She pinches his arm, hard.

And he laughs.

❄ 10 – You missed me

"You call this a date?"

"I said I was going to the store."

"Then why did you invite me?"

Isra rolls her eyes. "I specifically said, 'you don't need to come with me', and you said, 'I've decided I'm coming with you' and followed me here."

Khalid picks up a bag of apples. Inspects it. Throws it into the cart. "Couldn't have you come alone. You know, in case you missed me."

He's such a mess, she thinks. She doesn't even understand why the things he says make her smile. But they do. She knows what he wants to say though he doesn't always say them. She can read every emotion running through his mind just by looking at his eyes.

He's been following her around like a lost puppy ever since she came home from her parents.

He's been missing her. She wants to tell him she's been missing him too.

But surely…surely he must know.

❄ 11 – Honey eyes

Khalid watches his wife adjust her silk scarf. It's warm honey, the exact shade of his eyes. She claims it's her favourite. He wonders if that's why.

Isra turns to him. "How do I look?"

Like an angel.

Khalid tips his head onto his shoulder and examines her – like he hadn't just been staring the whole time.

"Sort of pretty...I guess."

Isra pulls a face and nudges him with a shoulder. He nudges her back.

"You're sort of pretty too," she says, her eyes glowing bright with humour.

"Yeah?"

"On a good day."

Khalid feels a smile inside of him, unfurling.

"There's this saying, 'beauty's in the eye of whoever looks at me-"

"-I don't think that's how the saying goes, Khalid."

"I think it is."

❋ 12 – How much sugar?

Love is in the subtle things:

When the Prophet Muhammad ﷺ and his wife, A'isha, would race and he'd intentionally lose, just to make her happy. When A'isha would insist on washing and combing his hair. When she drank a sip of water and the Prophet drank from the same spot. Khalid remembers how his dad would do this to his mum whenever they'd share a cup of chai. His sixteen-year-old self would roll his eyes at them, declaring his parents the epitome of puke-in-your-mouth cringe. And now...well. Perspectives were different now.

It's a Sunday afternoon, and Khalid is clearing out the garden for spring.

He's about to dig up some overgrown weeds when his eyes catch Isra waving at him from the kitchen window. She's holding up a pot of chai in her hands.

How much sugar? Isra mouths.

Khalid walks towards her. A lazy smile pulls at his lips.

"I don't mind," he says. "I'll take it after you sip."

❄ 13 – Wallet

"Feed me." Isra points at the fancy restaurant up the street. "In there."

Khalid glances at his almost empty wallet.

"Isra," he groans, resting his chin on her head. This was the fourth time. Today. She's robbing him. All his wife ever wants to do is eat.

❄ 14 – Favourite verse

It's past midnight, and Isra leans out of the bedroom balcony, her arms dangling loosely from the metal railing. The temperature has dropped considerably and she notices that there's a light touch of frost spreading over the world below. She can hear the tinkling of wind chimes, the call of an owl somewhere in the far distance, but these noises are eventually drowned out by the sound of Khalid's reciting, melodic and soft.

Isra recalls back to a *hadith* he'd once told her, that when someone recites the words of the Qur'an, their entire home lights up and shines to the people of the heavens, just as stars shine to the people of the earth.

"Khalid...what's your favourite verse?" Isra finds herself asking, and Khalid closes the book to meet her eyes.

"Too many. So many."

"But if you had to pick one."

There's a pause. Khalid sits back on his chair, thinking. Then, "O' content soul, come back to your Lord."

Isra looks over her shoulder. "Why's that your favourite?"

Khalid rakes his fingers through his dark hair, tousling its smooth surface. Stares ahead. "It's a verse where God calls upon righteous souls to enter into His paradise and spend the rest of eternity by His side." Khalid inhales a breath, his distant expression indicating his mind has gone somewhere far out of reach. A place beyond the sky he looks at. "When I die, these are words I long to hear. More than anything."

Isra doesn't think she knows a person more deserving of paradise than Khalid. He is goodness personified. Anyone who spends the length of a single day with him could see that.

Khalid continues to flick through the Qur'an, and Isra finds her gaze flickering upwards. The night's so dark, she can see the celestial body clearer than she has ever before. Something inside her stirs at the sight.

Those stars up there...they were the same stars that shone when prophets roamed the earth, that saw miracles happen, that used to glitter over *Rasulullah*'s home and have witnessed countless people come and go, over eras and aeons.

~

"Khalid." Her voice is quiet when it reaches his ear. "Do you want to know my favourite verse?"

Khalid looks up, his eyes crinkling. "I want to know yours."

"Exalted is He Who put constellations in the heavens, a radiant light, and an illuminating moon."

Of course his wife's favourite verse is going to be something related to the stars. She's an astrology fanatic. He should have called it.

"*Surah Furqan*?" he asks, yet already knowing he's right. "Chapter 25? Verse number 61?"

Isra huffs, but he catches the ghost of her smile when she turns away. "You're such a show-off."

❄ 15 – Experimenting

He's usually the one who cooks. He comes up with all these creative and healthy recipes that blow her mind with how good they look. Whilst Isra, of course, carries out the most important task of all: The tasting.

Today, however, she thought she'd surprise him with something truly special.

~

Khalid leans against the doorframe, hands in the pockets of his grey sweatpants, one ankle over the other.

"What's happening here?"

"I'm experimenting."

Khalid laughs as he uncrosses his legs and takes a step into the kitchen. "Let me guess, you're dissecting a rat?"

Isra looks down at the chicken on her tray and frowns.

Khalid can't stop his grin when he comes up behind her. He gives her shoulders a reassuring squeeze.

"You know I'm joking," he says into her ear, eyeing the burnt bird with its semi-cooked vegetables piled up around it. "It's looking amazing, Isra. Can't wait to try it."

When she cranes her neck to look up at him, and she gifts him with the sunniest smile he's ever seen, he thinks he'd probably eat a rat too – a dozen of them, if it made her this happy.

❄ 16 – Blueberry pancakes

He wakes up early morning to make her breakfast. Before he gets out of bed, he ruffles her hair. She says something indiscernible and opens her sleepy eyes. His broad silhouette floats across the room, in the golden hue.

"Stay," Isra calls out. He's already by the door.

Khalid looks back at her with a smile.

"I'm making blueberry pancakes," he says.

"Stay," she says anyway.

"I'll be right back," he laughs.

His silhouette floats down the corridor. The sound of his fading footsteps makes her feel something…

She has this urge to go after him.

Instead, she drifts back to sleep.

❄ 17 – Leave

She tries to smile. It looks so sad.

"Life's easier when you're here with me," she says. Then she glances at her feet, frowning.

"But when you leave,
It will be hard again."

❄ 18 – Living room floor

He's been away for months. A training course overseas that's lasting longer than it should have.

He thinks back to Isra. What she said before he left. His heart pounds. Khalid has never been good with words, he knew that. Yet he wishes he could find the right way to tell her, that after the end of a stressful day, he wants nothing more than to just sit and laugh with her on their living room floor.

❄ 19 – Welcome

Isra squeals when she hears the jingle of keys. She's racing down the stairs, racing into his arms, squeezing him so tight he can barely breathe out the name of her.

"Welcome back!"

Her voice drops. A whisper in his ear.

"This house hasn't felt like home
since you left."

Wow, he thinks. What am I gonna do with love like this.

❄ 20 – I'll take care of you

"Isra, I'm sick."

"*Inshallah* you'll get better, Khalid-*jaan*. I'll take care of you."

A sadness enters his eyes. "No, I-" He swallows. Looks down at his hands.

"It's not...it's not the type of sickness
I can recover from."

❄ 21 – Cry-baby

She has been quiet all day. Khalid finds her lying flat on the sofa, its fabric soaking up the flood of her tears.

Seeing her like this makes his chest hurt more than an asthma attack. He just wants to wrap his arms around her waist and press her back together. He wants to bring her out of the cold and into the warmth of his palms, as if he were a nest and she were a little bird.

But he doesn't know how to reach her.

Khalid sighs. Lifts her head gently and cradles it on his lap.

"Cry-baby Isra."

She turns so her face is buried into his stomach. "I'm not a cry-baby," she sniffs, and he has to swallow down a bubble of laughter because *God*, his wife's so cute. Even when she's sad.

"Yeah. You're right," he agrees softly, running his long fingers through her hair. "You're the bravest person I know."

It used to surprise him how emotional she could get, but he's come to understand it's mostly her empathy, how she feels things so deeply that sometimes even joy manages to wound her. It's who she is - his Isra. She's all heart.

Khalid can feel the front of his jumper dampening by the second. More tears. He doesn't comment, and Isra grows quiet once again. He thinks she might have fallen asleep, when her shaky voice breaks through the silence.

"What...what do you think our future's going to look like?"

There it is, Khalid thinks. Isra calls it 'The Distraction Game'. It's what they play when reality becomes too unbearable. So they push it aside

and re-write a world where everything's alright.

"I see our children five years from now," Khalid begins, slow at first. Testing the waters. He hears her take in a sharp breath, but then she's squeezing his arm, urging him to continue. So he does.

"They're standing in congregation beside me as they try to imitate each action of *salah*. They'll mess around and do it all wrong, but it'll be cute watching them try anyway. And then we'll hear your calls from the hallway, the scent of your burnt cooking will tickle our throats."

Isra makes a noise, halfway between a laugh and sob. His face softens.

"I can see these days coming…and it'll be the happiest we've ever been."

~

She doesn't want to forget any of this. The stories he tells. The way he's looking at her in this very moment. How, when he dips his head to kiss her forehead, the ache in her heart feels like it's being taken over by liquid light. She wants to hold onto everything so tight.

She wants to hold onto him

even tighter.

❄ 22 – In another life

In another life, she goes wherever he goes, and stays wherever he stays. They put up hammocks in springtime, he chases her by the hillside come fall. In that life, they start their mornings with leftover pizza and end their evenings with too many cups of coffee.

"We're so unhealthy," she complains, and he lifts the frown from her lips with a finger.

"Yeah, but at least we're happy."

In another life, he reads her to sleep and his hands get lost in the waves of her hair. In another life, they're always together. But not in this life.

No.

Just not in this one.

❄ 23 – Black hole

He touches her cheek. "Tell me something good."

"Like what?"

"Anything. Everything." What he means: *Please, distract me.*

"When I was a kid, I thought about space a lot. I'd come home with stacks of books. Everything from astrology to theories of the universe. But it was black holes that fascinated me most. A star so huge it collapsed in on itself. It's so massive that not even light can escape its gravity, which is why it's almost perfectly black. I read somewhere that time slows near one. And inside a black hole time stops. Completely." Isra exhales so deeply her shoulders sag.

"You know, Khalid," she says, slumping down on her chair. "I wish we were floating in the centre of a black hole."

❄ 24 – The other side

"O' content soul, come back to your Lord."

Has the time come already?
For him to cross that bridge?

~

He is going to die.

The thought settles in his blood like poison, like an aftertaste he can't get rid of, like a haunting in the back of his mind.

He is going to die,
and he doesn't know if death will find in him
a willing companion.

~

"I wish we had more time together." She breathes into his shoulder.

"I wanted to talk to you about the beginning of everything."

~

He shatters infinitely. He spills blood and it runs through the length of everything.

But Isra: Who used to look at him like he was capable of anything. Like if he held his hands together, he could bond the universe. Like if he held his arms apart, he could take flight.

So maybe he can't take showers by himself anymore, and maybe most nights he wakes up heaving. And standing upright gives him the same sickness as heights.

But for the way she looks at him – for her,
he can hang on
till the emergence of morning.

~

They share this deep sadness between them, like falling into the jaws of an open fire. A pain so radiant it cuts through all others.

"What will I do without you?"

Khalid gazes at Isra, with his hollow cheeks and dark under eyes, tinged with love.

"Everything you did before me," he replies, catching her tears with his thumb.

"And I'll be there
waiting for you on the other side."

~

For the people of this world, the highest declaration of love is mentioned in their wedding vows, '*till death do us apart*' - I'll love you and take care of you up until my last breath.

As for Muslims, Khalid knows their love and affection for their spouses are not buried along with them in death, but instead it lives on, until they are reunited again in *Al-Jannah.*

I will love you,
twice.
Once in this world
and once again
in Paradise.

❄ 25 – I miss you

"I miss you," she says. It's a whisper he almost can't catch.

"I'm right here," he says, tracing her furrowed brows. "Isra, I'm right here."

But she shakes her head. Even as he pulls her closer, even as she falls back asleep, she shakes her head.

❄ 26 – The Prophet

He says, "I always think about the Prophet Muhammad ﷺ and A'isha, where he died with his head resting on her chest.
Perhaps that's my final wish
- it always was."

❄ 27 – I'll be here

He doesn't talk. Doesn't eat. Mostly drifting in and out of consciousness whilst she sits by him.

Night falls. The sun rises.
Winter melts into spring.

He doesn't get better.

She sits by him.
And her mind takes her back...

...Khalid lifting himself over a fence to pick her wildflowers. Her smearing blueberries on his face like it's war paint, whilst he naps peacefully
under the sky. Khalid on the roof,
framed by the sun.
His gaze on her, like she's both a marvel and a wonder.
His warm hands
brushing her cheek.

She looks at him now and he's an echo of what he'd been. Fragile and thin. A weakness in him she's never witnessed before. All ash and ice and emptiness.

"I'll be here every night," she tells him, voice so soft, so tortured, "to keep you warm. I'll talk to you until I can't keep my eyes open."

"Ignore the darkness," she whispers.

A single tear
drops on his hand.

"Think of me instead."

And he feels it.

I'm sorry, Isra he wants to say to her.

I'm sorry.

❄ 28 – Hospital

He crushes her against the dying thud of his chest
and he thanks her
for the life and the memories and the heartache,
for planting herself so deep in his heart
that it left no room for the darkness to grow.
And he thanks her
for gifting him with all her sunny smiles, especially on
days when he had none to offer himself,
and for holding onto him so tightly
throughout the suffering,
during all those long and bleak weeks he'd spent in the
hospital,
and for refusing to let go of his hand
even when the doctors had asked her
many times
to leave.

❄ 29 – Letters to Khalid

Khalid,
I watched you lying on the hospital bed.
There wasn't even an atom's weight of life in you.
And I remember how I had to press my hands against
your chest
every few minutes
to convince myself that you were somehow
still breathing.
I brought your hands to my lips. I remember them being
so cold.
I had said, "I wish you had brought me your pain." My
voice cracked.
I kissed your fingertips.
"And I would have traded them for all my joy."
And when I cried, uncontrollably,
I didn't have to worry

that I'd wake you from your slumber.

Time

passes…

❄ 30 – Letters to Khalid

Come back. Come back and shout at me. Come back and fight with me. Come back and break my heart,
if you want.
Just come back.

❋ 31 – Letters to Khalid

I left the window open all night
but even the wind
couldn't fill your absence.

❄ 32 – A list of things that hurt:

- the smell of blueberry pancakes
- ~~hearing someone utter~~ your name
- fresh flowers in cemeteries
- dreams in which you're alive
- waking up from them

❄ 33 – Letters to Khalid

It would be nice if I could forget how you smelt - or if that black *thobe* my brother wears didn't remind me of you (you brought it for him last winter). I can't go back to that pretty mosque in green avenue or our favourite bookstore or sleep alone in the dark anymore. I haven't stepped foot inside our house for a month. I'm sorry I can't. The ghost of you still lingers on those walls.
But like I tell myself I'm getting better at dealing with your loss. And then somebody smiles in a certain way, or they crack a lame joke that gets me laughing
just like you used to.
And there you are again, all in my head.
And I'm back there again.
Back to missing you.

❋ 34 – Letters to Khalid

I have stayed up so many nights asking God: How will I survive this missing? How do others do it? Loved ones die all the time. Every day. Every waking hour. There are families all over the world staring at beds that are no longer slept in, clothes that are no longer worn. There are women cooking meals for their children, men waking up early for work, there are children riding their bikes to school, while inside, their hearts are breaking. For years. For their whole lives. I don't believe time heals. I don't want it to.

If I heal, doesn't that mean I've already accepted a world without you in it?

❋ 35 – Mother

"I miss him, mum."

And when tears would spill from my cheeks at the thought of him,

she would whisper, "come here, Isra-*jaan*." And I'd feel her arms wrapping around me, the same arms that held me in infancy.

And I find my head resting against her chest, enveloped in all her love, her motherly tenderness.

How is it, that after all these years
my mother's arms
still felt like the safest place in both heaven and earth?

❄ 36 – Forget

They say time. They say it heals. The days come. The days go. My heart doesn't understand.

Listen, my heart tells me. *You can't forget him. Maybe after all this time,*
he will come back.

❄ 37 – A memory

"The Prophet once said, 'you will be with the one you love'. Remember this always," Khalid whispered. "Even when I'm gone.
Remember it."

❄ 38 – Letters to Khalid

I remember once I had asked you if you were afraid of dying.
You had answered, "why should we fear it
when it's the only reality past this life?
Every soul shall taste death, Isra.
We're not supposed to stay here forever."

Now that you're lying beneath the darkness of the earth, are you afraid, Khalid? Do you miss the warmth of the sun that once grazed your face? Does it get lonely there?

I can only wonder.

❋ 39 – Letters to Khalid

I shook when I thought about that day.
Felt scared to the nerves of me.
I used to wake up panting after dreaming about how you had died again.
I've lost a lot of things over the past year. My pride, my dreams, my mind.
You.
I wake up and I make a different dream.
Not of your death.
No.
I dream of your life instead. The time we spent. The years we shared.
I wake up alone
but I don't wake up cold.
Yes. You're gone. And I survived that. And something in that realisation
makes me feel stronger
than I was before.

❄ 40 – Solace

The clouds are the colour of cotton candy. The air is sweet. The winter sun is a caress on her cheek. The wind is cold, but the sort of cold that carries thoughts away into solace. She's surrounded by bare-branched trees. Here, everything is beautiful.

Here,
nothing hurts.

❄ 41 – Letters to Khalid / a goodbye

Dear Khalid,
I've realised that there are endings sadder than ours. Some lovers do not even get to embrace, exchange *I love yous* or say goodbye to one another. And we were able to do all those things.
So I write my final letter to you, not because I don't grieve you still, but because I've finally learnt how to breathe on my own again. I can wake up every morning and appreciate life like I used to. Everything under the sun and moon no longer leaves me in agony.
And I know that someday
we'll get to be together again, underneath the bluest of skies, amongst the vibrant meadows of a paradise we once so longingly dreamt of. I know that however beautiful I imagine our reunion to be, God will make it all the more sweeter.

With hope at last,
Isra.

"we are all souls,
my love,
and when you fell
you came to be a part of this world,
and when you are taken,
my love,
i know you will rise again.
to beyond the stars you'll go
to a heaven that calls for you.
until we meet again,
until
we meet again."

(Isra's ode to Khalid
- found in her final letter)

Heaven's Scent

"But it is in the province of religion,
of philosophy, of pure poetry only,
to go beyond life, beyond time, into eternity."

—Alfred de Vigny

And you sat there in the dark
limbs shaking in the storm
crying,
"O' my Lord
please,
take me to a place
where my heart will stop hurting."

- O' Light of those who are lonely in the darkness,
heal the broken-hearted.

Life pales,
people sail away
but Your presence prevails.
How I can feel it
even during
my most lonely days.

And I think of You
when the morning is half awake
and the sun has barely begun
creeping across the horizon.

- *As-Salam, The Giver of peace*

Tell your mountains
about your God
and watch them crumble
to their dust.

I swear
when you return to Him again
everywhere you go it feels like
flowers are blooming,
birds are singing.
You feel lighter
like you're suspended in air
and the season of winter
that had once settled into your heart
is overtaken
by a breathless spring.
It feels like rebirth
and new beginnings.
Like life starting
all over again.

He knows what you feel
in the deepness of your heart
when in the night,
your loneliness is so heavy
it crushes you,
as if the sky itself has swooped down
to smother you in its cold arms.

Speak to Him.
He's so close.

If only you knew.

All these bad days I could have avoided,
if I had simply chosen
to love You more.

You've been looking so tired and gloomy lately
like you've been battling the world
and the world had won.

I stopped by to ask if you were alright.

"I'm fine" you tried for a smile
and the sight of it was so heart-breaking,
I didn't think all the world's oceans
could fill the emptiness in your heart.

- I hope one day
you learn to have faith in God again.

I did not fall in love with You,
my Lord.

I *rose* in it.

My Lord
how I burn
how I burn with such longing
to leave all worldly things behind,
and fly
back to You.

Don't call her yours out of ownership.
Call her yours because she is part of you,
like a limb
like Eve
sprouting from the ribs of Adam.
Two beautiful halves
to one glorious whole.

- This is *love*

There is a place
where there are gardens grander
than the expanse of this earth.
An immortal land of milk and honey,
where death can never find you
and every soul will be
with the one it loves.

Wait for me there.

"The next life will be kinder to you," I say.

"Over there, they'll know what I know - have always known. That you were too good for this world and all that was in it."

"And how do you know that?"

Then, a silence.

Lingering.

You could hear the birds chirping the first melodies of sunrise.

"Because," I begin, glancing up at the light piercing through the horizon,

"God always rewards those who endure."

What is love?

When Abu Bakr didn't move an
inch when his foot was bitten into
by a snake, because The Prophet ﷺ
was sleeping peacefully on his lap.

What is love?

When Bilal left the illuminated city
of Medina after The Prophet ﷺ
died, because everything in that
city reminded him of his beloved ﷺ.

What is love?

When Ali came to Medina with his
feet swollen due to walking such a
distance, and The Prophet ﷺ cried
when looking at them
and went to massage his feet.

This.
This is *love.*

And with shaky hands,
Abu Bakr lifted the white cloth
from the illuminated face
of his most beloved.
Kissing his blessed forehead
he whispered
with such sadness and sorrow,

"O messenger of God.
How blessed was your life,
and how beatific
is your death."

- Death of The Prophet

You're going to realise it one day - that happiness was never about your job or your degree or your wealth. Happiness was never about following in the footsteps of all of those who are more successful than you; it was never about trying to please people. One day, you're going to see it - that happiness was always the way your mother called your name when you returned home after so long, the way you ran after your siblings in the park whilst the sun was shining down on you, the days your family gathered as one on a single table filled with warm homemade food, so that you could break your fast together. Happiness was the sweetness you felt in *salah* when your faith was at its peak. It was looking outside of your window on rainy nights and realising how lucky you were to be alive like this. These small things that you take for granted now, you will look back to someday. And you will realise. This was it. This moment now. Was when you were the happiest.

Always, over and over
these days and nights will come:
The hollowness to your bone
discovering the ache of love lost,
the pain of separation,
stricken soar with ailments.
But your Lord will not leave you in this sorry state.

Rise to feel the heat of the sun
on your back.
The wind that embraces you
like a mother's warm hug.

Oh sweetheart,
you are alive.
Learn to fall in love
with life again.

I am Your pilgrim.
I have crossed snowstorm and desert
mountains
bridges

to reach You.

The stars in the sky don't sit there
because we're deserving of it.
They're there because He is The Lord of the worlds
and holds all things together in place.
The earth is still revolving
and your heart is still beating
because His Mercy upon you is unfailing.
There is always hope until the sun rises
from where it sets.
There is a chance to be reborn
with every breath that you take.
And know on the mornings in which you rise
is only God presenting you with a new beginning,
a blank canvas,
twenty-four hours, yours for the taking,
so that you may try
all over again.

The despair of the world grows on you like moss
and you wake in the night to the feeling
of its gripping.
Go and lie down where the forest beckons.
Where water stills
and fields stretch like a blanket over all things.
Become lost again,
in the remembrance of a time
where mankind slept on beds of ferns and flowers,
under the motionless blue
of fallen skies.
Come into the peace of the wild

calling you back
to yourself.

You hold so much pain, don't you?
I know,
I know.
But there is Someone Who is aware of your pain,
witnesses your tears,
Who hears your cries,
even in silence.
And He is willing to listen to the grievances
of your heart
if you are only willing
to tell them to Him.

You stomp across the earth
with so much arrogance.
Forgetting that she will
take you back someday,
grow over you,
and leave you forgotten.

"Do not walk proudly on the earth;
your feet cannot tear apart the earth
nor are you as tall as the mountains."
— Qur'an, 17:37

How strange is *dunya?*
When in one moment
you could be shining
with the radiance
of early morning,

and then suddenly
you find yourself
pouring down with rain.

"When my soul passes
what legacies shall I leave behind?"

Let it be kindness.
Let it be softness.
Let the world lament over their loss
for a soul that came to them
walking on rose petals,

and left them drowning in grief
upon his death.

And my *duas*, they follow you
through the skyless night of the street,
like the memory of a bird you once had
that died.

So will you remember me
my friend,
when I'm gone?

Enter my prayers, then.
Until my tongue only remembers
the shape of your name.
You'll be sheltered as long as I live.

- Protect them through prayers,
and let God handle the rest.

Your *rooh* is more beautiful
than your face

but I could write ballads
about both.

I want to be the personification of a child
curling into your stomach and laying rest there,
the wonder of treading through ancient temples
and holy grounds;
the feeling of crawling into bed
after a long night's journey,
and the gentle touch of your mother's hands.
I want to be the softness of the sky
before it awakens, possess all the fragrance
of a *fajr's* breeze;
to be a meadow
you never want to stop running through,
coloured in all the hues of autumn leaves.
I want to be the embodiment of Friday when the streets
fill with the hum of evening prayers,
and the first sip of your favourite chamomile tea;
to be the entrance of a heaven that whispers,
"finally,
you've come home to me."

Dear sorrows of my heart
He put you inside of me
to teach me valuable lessons.
So
teach me of them.

I am ready to learn.

Long ago, you were wounded.
Learnt that you will find no rest in this world.
No rest.
But you will find your way home someday,
my friend
to a place where your soul had once existed.
A place where you can take off your armour
and live a life after the agony,
as if you had never tasted
the bitterness of yesterday.

When I was five, I couldn't doze off if my father wasn't beside me.
When I was seven, I'd wait by the window until he came home.
When I was thirteen, wearing his nightgown made me feel like the safest creature in all the world.
At fifteen, I handed all of my fears over to him
and watched him break them into pieces.

They say adulthood is a land where you have to look out for yourself. But they haven't met my father.
Seven years later and there he is,
standing like a mountain behind me.
Tall and sturdy and unshakable.

He makes me breakfast when he finds me rummaging through the kitchen cupboards early morning. Drives me to the ends of the country, says,
"no daughter of mine will wait at bus stops when I have a car."

When the darkness hounds me, he stands beside my door and prays in words I don't understand.
But they sound like an ocean of flowers,
all blooming.
I keep them locked away in the crevice of my heart.

I hug him tight that winter he falls ill.
The thought of being without him is a needle in my throat. An open wound unhealing.

"Are you praying for me?" he asks, voice weakening
and hoarse.

I rest my head on his frail shoulder.
"Yes, baba."
Hero to all my stories,
whose skin's the colour of wet sand.
When I was younger I thought he built our house
with his own two calloused hands.

"I always am."

Why do you wonder if they love you back? When she carried you in the darkness of her womb for nine months. When she worries if you haven't eaten and stays up late till you return home safe and sound. When he works late shifts and rises before the sun even on mornings when sleep desperately clings to the corners of his eyes. When he does this so you can live a life of comfort and ease. When he buys you your favourite food and checks to see if you're sleeping soundly at night.
They might not tell you they love you,
but they have been showing you they do
all their lives.

- How immigrant parents say *I love you.*

When you were hurt
they swept you up
like a bundle in their arms
and softly pressed their lips to every wound.

So say:
O' *my Lord,*
have mercy upon my parents,
for they raised me when I
was small.

How she has loved you.
How she would have moved the earth to stand beside you.
How she has chased the fear out of your nightmares and into the light,
so you could sleep in peace at night.
How she would have cut out the fruits of her heart
if it meant she could keep you happy.

Who is she, you wonder?
Why,
she is your mother.

Mother is the twilight
that reminds you morning is close.
She is the voice that pulls you out of all your night tremors,
and the lighthouse that guides you home
when you're lost.

She is every safe
and wholesome thing.

Your mother cares,
she cares for miles and miles.
Her love for you is so big
it should have its own currency,
its own capital city,
and its own continent.

To hear her voice above the ruins of the day.
I find courage in the spring
that blossoms from her face.
The absence of her drinks me dry.

Oh mother,
you are my heart and eyes.

I will wrap you up
and hold you close
so hurt can never utter
the name of you.

- Mother

In a world that is already hurting,
painted and shrouded with aching,
can't we be soft with one another?
Can't we tend to each other's wounds
and become the spring
that melts away each other's winters?

- Because not everyone is happy
and everybody needs a little care.

When the world started to tarnish his spirit
and the weight on his shoulders
wore him to his knees,
he would pick himself up and say,
"endure,
my heart,
for you have endured a far worse thing
than this."

Go to the gardens
when you need to be reminded
that beautiful things
take time to grow.

And when the sadness
that I have come to loathe so much
comes to knock on your door,
  don't open it.

Remind her that you're loved
and so full of it
that there's no room inside of you
for her to reside in
  anymore.

The days we open the windows
to let in the *fajr* breeze,
when we visit the mountain peaks
and lie there carefree,
and we break our fast as the sun dips
into sea
these are the days that I long for.

When he held his daughter
for the first time

he wondered what his arms were for
          other than to hold her

and what his heart was for
          other than to love her.

Your daughter,
she is a city sleeping in a cot before you, warm and bright and familiar, streetlights yawning and stretching, and you have never
you have never
you have never loved a being like this.
A mountain is moving somewhere inside you, and her tiny handprints are all over it.
Here is the proof,
in the fractured morning,
when you are too tired and too sad,
her crying is what pushes your foot off of the bed. She is the fight in you, what keeps you going, what stops the shipwreck floating in your chest.
When they ask you what your favourite moment is, you will say her.
When I hold her.
When I am with her.

- A father's anchor

I will root myself like a tree
and turn the soil over with my bare hands
to steady the earth beneath her.

I'll become the kind of mother
who can make the stars fit inside
her tiny palms.

- To my daughter

So you've just found the scarf your grandmother used to wear, and you swear you can hear her laughter from down the hall. Your fingers trace the slightly worn fabric. You remember all the times you hugged her when she wore it.

You bring it to your face, and somehow it still smells like her.
You can't believe it still smells like her.

You're sitting on her bed, holding her scarf between your clammy palms, and your throat closes up because she is far and gone, but you smile because a piece of her still remains here with you.

For a moment when the wind
picks up
and the trees rustle,
I'm standing beside your grave,
I realise the extent of my sorrow.

I loved you so much
it was like I was practically crying out:
Here's the location of the soul I have cared for,
buried beneath the earth.

And here lies the source of all beauty and happiness,
now reduced
to dust and bone.

- Grandma, some losses are greater than others.
You were one.

I have so much grief inside of me, I whisper.
Where do I put it all?

Carry it, society orders.
Carry it.
For what does it mean to be a woman
other than to endure?

It angered her that her purpose in life
has been reduced to simply looking beautiful,
always,
and her value as a person depended entirely
on how desirable she was to a man.

- You deserve to be judged by the quality of your person rather than the skin you're in. You deserve to be a person, wholly, without regard to appearances. I wish this is what society would teach our women.

How do I tell you:
Run.
That the blade of him isn't there for fun.
You try to cover up the marks he left
on your skin.
Why do you stay with a man
that doesn't make you feel safe with him?

You say no, it's fine,
he won't do it again.
Don't worry.
I'm fine.
It's just men being men.

I love you. I do.
My darling sister,
my night sky,
friend since forever.
I cried the hardest on your wedding day,
remember?

But tell me,
how do I save you from this?
When you're not even willing
to save yourself.

- Lovers do not leave bruises.
They heal them.

This body that absorbs me
I beg it:
Can you rebuild yourself from clay once more.
Make beautiful what is
so ugly.
Smooth out the rougher edges, kick out
all the things I say do not belong.

My body sits up, holds me at arm's length.
Says,
we *will build for you muscles*
that will make you sturdy.
Paint you proudly in ivory scars.
Let the world relearn
the meaning of survival.

There will come better days
when your limbs won't be cursed
for the bundle that they carry, these stretch marks for
the lands they have colonised.

You will say,
thank God for
the wide expanse of my hips.
Hills I did not
die upon
but instead found peace between.

Plucking golden ripe mangoes
from branches of blooming trees.
Teeth bursting into their flesh
tender and sweet.

Bright cotton sarees dancing against the wind.
The sound of bangles clinking together
singing, singing, singing.

Long silk hair glistening
under sunlight.
Running through wild jungles and green
watery rice fields.
Cold wind slapping against our wet skin.

Swimming in deep flowing rivers, stepping through
creaking old bridges.

Catching the scent of our mothers cooking
leading us back to our homes.

- Motherland

I take you by the hand.

I show you the jackfruit trees I used to climb as a child
and the spot where I fell and broke my knee.

I show you the fish swimming beneath the folds of the
sea and teach you how to catch them,
just like how my grandfather taught me.

This is my motherland. Where I grew up and lived and
breathed.

This is a special part of me,
that I want you to meet.

I will remember you like this:
How you would cover my body with yours
like it was instinct
when bombs fell from the sky
like burning stars.
Those days when we barely had scraps to eat
you'd insist you weren't hungry,
and hand-fed me all your shares.

That morning
when we decided that freedom
wasn't a word that can be captured
- that it can only be chased after.

And that final moment
when you were shot to the head
with a single bullet,
and fell into my arms
soaking in warm crimson blood.

"Remember me"
was the last thing you had whispered

but tell me...
how could I ever forget?

- Into the lands of war

How I lost you...
amidst the ceaseless firing of bullets
under the endless falling of bombs
beneath the rubbles of another collapse
between the sorrow of losing a loved one
and the relief of returning to your Lord.
I know I won't be seeing you in this life again
but if I make it to *Jannah*
I will look for you

and I will listen to all your unfinished stories.

O, child of the diaspora,
what is the tongue of your lullabies?
What is the dialect of your people?
What letters do you write in?
And which do you remember?
What is it to have a homeland that does not bite?

We have felt as uprooted in our motherland as we do here. Our father's birthplace is bitter cold to the touch, our grandmother is from a country that is no longer on the map.

We are believers, the children of believers.
We are refugees, the children of refugees.
Our feet hit the ground running.
Even now the urge to flee crackles in our blood.
Perhaps you can answer us.
What is it to have tranquillity in physical space? A safe haven on solid ground?

Don't you know we broke our mouths to learn your language? To taste a better life?

Two decades have passed, and we still remember the months it took on boat to reach here. To arrive. Bruised, broken and a heart swelling with hope - that you may accept us. For we have lost the place we once called home.

Home is not a place, it's a feeling

Never understood the saying
'home is not a place, it's a feeling'
until I'm laughing so hard at my sister's jokes.
We're sprawled out on the couch, facing each other,
smiling like idiots, mouths stretched so wide
our cheeks ache from the strain of it.

Never felt more at home than during those long car
journeys
when it's just me and my father.
I'd listen to him retell tales of childhood,
a nostalgic smile
grazing his worn face.
His eyes tear up
a little
at the mention of his parents.
It makes me appreciate that much more
all that I have.

Never felt more at home than the nights
I stay up with my mother.
The world is fast asleep,
and the soft sound of her reciting Qur'an
seems to be the only thing that can be heard for miles.

It's within the pockets of these moments that I finally understood. I finally understand.
It's never been the house that's made the home.
But always the people in it.

You ask me at night
for stories of happy endings.

Us, I begin
stretched beneath the starlit skies
of His holy heaven.

Days of November
Longing has a season.
It's called winter.

The Loving

Poems are not always for lovers.
Our friendship takes the direction of my longing
and I cannot set you down
like a book with dog-eared pages,
tattered cover
and frayed spine.
I write you this poem on a November morning of memory
whilst you're tucked into a little apartment
some hundred miles away.
I want to ask if you've seen it
- the snow we once viewed together.
The trees cloaked in white sheets
and flowers bent underground.
I fear that the world might end
before we meet again
or share a cup of coffee in this cold and busy city,
or before I get to utter the words
of how much your company has meant to me.

I want it all with you. The cottage overlooking fields of evergreens. I want the lavish plants and us basking beneath the morning light. I want the peace in you; the soft smiles and children's laughter, watching how the sun draws its patterns across your face, whilst you sleep warm next to me. We can't have it all, I know that, but humour me.
We can't have it,
I know,
but we can have most of it.

- I lie awake
waiting for these days to reach us.

Aalam-Al-Arwah

My eyes are closed and I'm almost asleep when I hear you say, "you make me feel so nostalgic."

"What do you mean?" I yawn, squinting at your direction. You are nothing but a shadow in the dark.

You reply, "I feel like I've known you for a thousand years," the floorboards creak and then the sofa dips under your weight, "but all those memories we've had together, they've been lost. Forgotten."

You're sitting beside me and when I shift to the left, our shoulders brush. "Have you heard the story of *Aalam-Al-Arwah*?" I ask. "Our past life?"

I can't see your face, but I can hear the smile in your voice when you say, "tell me about it."

"The Prophet ﷺ mentioned in a *hadith* that souls who knew each other in the land of souls would find each other in this world too, and souls who developed animosity there would fail to get along and eventually separate." I raise the blanket until it covers you too, and pull it tightly around us. "It must be why, when we meet certain people, we're overcome with this - this unexplainable feeling that we've *met them* somewhere before, or we've known them. All our lives."

Faint silvery light streams through the cracks between the blinders and I angle my head, studying your profile in the moonlight.

You're transfixed, looking at me like I'm one of those wise old men that sit near campfires and narrate tales of buried history and mystic past.

"I think...the same could be said for those moments when you miss someone you've never met," I continue. "It's our soul yearning for those other souls, waiting for them to show up in our life."

Don't you think it's beautiful? I want to say, *to have known each other before birth, before time.*

"Thank you," you whisper in the dark, a thousand years later. Light-years have passed - or at least it feels like it, in the haze of my mind that floats on the edge of consciousness.

"For what?"

A pause. I can hear your heart pounding in the silence. A hummingbird's trapped somewhere inside your chest.

"For finding me," you finally draw out. "For showing up."

The hazel forest of your eyes soften when I take your hand.

You lace your fingers through mine. "I'm grateful to have known you in my past life." Pressing our joint hands to your chest, you say, "and it's been an honour to have met you again in this one."

I look at you
and feel a future where we live
with our rescued pets and greenhouses.
Painting our bedroom the bluest of blues
because I know it's your favourite.
I'll spend all my time finding ways to fill up your life.
To hear your soft sighs at sundown.
To find your books left by my nightstand.
Listen to raindrops bumping onto rooftops,
with your head that rests,
always,
in the crooks of my shoulder.

- I could make you happy

I saw you in my dreams last night,
and the night before that. You missed me, you were happy to see me. You took me to see a lake at the edge of the forest. We sat there and spoke about nothing and everything. I don't know why I have dreams like that. Where you're so real
it's like I can almost feel the heat of your palms
when I reach for them.

I've been here
inside of your heart before.

I recognise that tree,
watched you beneath
its peaches.

Handed you my love
beside

that riverbend.

Listen,
you have entered into all of my night prayers.

Listen,
I am thankful we are alive on this earth
in the same moment.

Believe me, it's true,
I don't believe I've met someone
who even compares to you.

You show me beautiful things
that I've never thought to look for.

I'm happier just knowing you,
breathing the same air as you.

And maybe it's late,
and maybe that's why I've become so sentimental,

but truth is truer at night, and the truth is,
I am in awe.
Of you.

I hope that's okay.

I was lonely in the forest,
sad,
with darkness falling over me.
But then you barged in through the trees,
sunlight
streaming in from behind you.

Come with me
you had said.

And I did.

- Had another dream about you.

I counted the days, counted the miles,
the oceans, the languages
that come
between us

until there you were,
standing against my door
asking
if I'd come with you
yet already knowing
that I would follow you anywhere.

- Close the distance.
It only hurts when we're apart.

When they asked,
"what is heaven in your language?"
I pronounced your name.

And when I die,
I will tell them to imbed my scent
into the walls of every room
that has ever made you feel alone.

I met you and reconciled with the world
and pardoned the absentees.
I have excused all my enemies.
Made peace with those who have hurt me.

Since I met you
even my anger
turns to honey.
And I see that there is nothing that can cause me
unhappiness,
except your unhappiness.

When did your name change
from a proper noun to a
prayer? That's all I whisper,
the whole day long.

After the sky has grown tired
and the merchants
have closed down their busy stalls,
the birds of me
shall return
once more
to the trees of you.

- Coming home

Lighthouse Keeper

Can you take the pain and go somewhere? Can you make it a journey? Someday you will go with no last words or final promises, in a ship that will sail by night without others following. You will drift through the waves in slow motion until you reach land.

She will be standing there on the coast, bearing a torch that will almost blind you.

Who are you? she'll demand. *Why have you come here?*

For peace, you'll say, and the exhaustion on your face will ring so true she'll have to believe you.

It will seem to you that her eyes, whose colour you connot fathom in the slightest, regard you for an infinite time.

I live in that lighthouse, she'll say, and lift her chin towards a tall building that sits on top of a mighty cliff.

Follow me, before you freeze to death.

She is deep shrinking shyness, she is fear of being touched. Moves away when you come near her like robins on a branch. She will build bricks around her body, but you are slow creeping ivy. Ice-breaker. Gift-wrap. When she asks you three weeks later why you haven't left yet you'll give her sheepish smiles and a one-shouldered shrug.

Melancholic endings, cities where other people have laid you bare. You are kept up late by your neighbour's foghorn voice and some marital affair. You are the blade of a knife meeting a ribcage, sinking. You are afraid of long nights. You are afraid of front doors slamming. You are afraid that if she takes a peek at your wrapping, she will see that the gift comes empty.

She is quick-witted. She is clever. Understands the laws of tide and nature. Picks up the subtle changes in the weather. One day rushes into your cabin and shouts, *quick! There is a storm coming.*

She is raincloud lungs and selkie fins. You are a small-bodied fish and she is the entire ocean. She is the protector dragon, the centre of the fire. You watch her stop death and shipwreck with her beacon of light and sheer willpower. She teaches you how to keep lanterns burning as brightly and clearly as possible. You show her the veins in your arm and how they're still pulsing. You could be death, could be end, could be mourning. But she has given you purpose, direction, some meaning.

Thank you for letting me stay here, you'll tell her when you pass her in the kitchen. You'll be setting the table and she'll be boiling crabs' skin. She won't meet your eyes, but she'll be almost smiling.

Well, you and I, she'll admit, *we make a good team.*

The moon rises. The sun sinks. You will be looking around the lighthouse when you hear the sound of sobbing. You'll find her in the same clothes, tear-stained and crumpled in her bathtub. You'll get her out, tuck her under the quilts she told you her grandmother sew. They smell like roses and lavender. You won't sleep here. You'll curl up in the corner of the lantern room watching ships come and go in the dark. You are still nocturnal tenancies; you are still twilight awakening. Your afternoon comes at three in the morning.

You will go back and gentle-help her, feeding her arms into the sleeves of a sweater, quiet hands untangling her hair and helping her downstairs and then preparing a small meal you know she won't eat.

You will be simple ways. You will not push her. You are steady-get-to-know-her. The months pass, you do not pressure. And she won't ask you to leave her either. You are lightweight, you are a feather. The bags under your eyes don't get any thicker. You knock on the doors of sleep and it lets you enter.

On a broken-glass evening too loud for your silence, she will drag you to the empty rocky beach. You both sit there while the water laps at your feet. Hailstones fall and she will toss her coat over you both, blocking out the entire world.

Her laughter, your new favourite sound, you would want to bottle it up and drink it by the gallon.

Save it for days when you need to hear it most.

And she does get better. And she will be curled up by the fireplace asking you about home, about shelter.

I don't know, you will answer. *I'm still searching for it.*

And she will nod and look away and her smile will falter.

It will be like living in a fevered dream with her. The way she will just go on and coat your entire heart with honey and cream without even realising it. When she laughs at everything you say, you'll melt like pancake batter. She will steal all your comfortable clothes even though they'll never fit her. But you won't mind when they come back smelling like her - mint leaves, vanilla, and a hint of saltwater. Pant leg and shirt sleeves rolled up since she's ten miles shorter.

She is your lighthouse keeper. Your escape key. You were lost in the sea of unrest and her light guided you to safety. When she reads you to sleep you are floating, you are sunbeam. She has cracked you open like a spine and found each scar inside you worthy.

If she asks about home, you will have your answer, and it will be: *Wherever you live and sit and breathe. Wherever you are - that's where my hearts at peace.*

If there was no kindness in your old home, we will fill it in ours, and we will give it walls, and we will furnish it with soft, wooden interior, from the inside out, and we will lock our doors to keep the anger away. To ward off the memories of your father's rowdy footsteps and your mother's piercing screams.

Someday,
we will raise a family in a place you could not mistake for any home
you've ever been in.
And it will be named
the safest place
you've ever known.

If only we were trees
growing in some forgotten corner
of the forest.

There, nothing could ever touch us,
there, we're left to grow - to intertwine.
My roots against your roots
forever.

You left an empty packet of dried mango
pieces next to my bed.
That's really all I wanted to say.
This isn't a poem as much as it is
a thank you note
for always leaving your mess somewhere
so I can look at it.
For leaving your lip stains
on my coffee mug
so sweet
I can't bear to clean it up
right away.
For giving me so many parts of yourself
to cling onto
when you're away.

There is a little house somewhere,
surrounded by honeysuckle and grapevines.
The warm kitchen light is glowing
 - the microwave song
hot coffee spills
the piecing together of things leftover
from night.

Somewhere I am sitting with you
in stillness,
mindlessly looping an arm
around your waist

like how the mountains
pull the sun around them,
warmed by her embrace.

The oldest story

The first time you meet,
it's in your back garden.
Your mother invites his family over for tea.
He's sitting on your childhood swing-set,
the summer sun setting down,
casting him in gold.

The eleventh time you meet,
you've accidentally hit him with a snowball
and he's shaking the snow out of his hair.
His eyes glint in the distance when he grabs a fistful
from the ground.
"You have ten seconds to run," he warns.
And you set off,
screaming with laughter.

The twentieth time you meet,
it's at his mother's funeral.
He's knelt on the floor,
face buried into his brother's shirt.
You can't see his expression,
but his shaking limbs
speak enough of his loss.

The thirty-fourth time you meet,
he's outside your apartment complex,

holding up a bag of Belgian pastries in one hand.
"These were mum's favourite," he murmurs.
"I thought you might like some."

The forty-first time you meet,
you're both lying on the grass at dawn
and he's telling you how desperately
he wants to leave.
"Everything in this town reminds me of her.
Turns out that's a huge problem for me."

The fiftieth time you meet,
it's at the airport.
You're standing face to face,
neither of you knowing what to say.
"You've been a good friend." He taps your nose,
smiling. "Don't miss me too much."

The last time you meet,
it's on the eve of his wedding.
Finally, the radiance of bliss
touches his bronze skin.
He catches your eyes before you exit the building.
G*oodbye* they seem to be saying,
and your chest tightens
into a knot.
It's been a pleasure to have known you.
You give him a small wave, heart breaking.
Stay happy.
Stay well.

It doesn't matter if some days
you feel like vibrant blossoms
budding from the earth.

And other days
you feel like rotting weeds - barely surviving.

I shall water both. I shall nurture both.
And I shall love both versions of you
just the same.

Play fights about nothing. Inside jokes that make us both wheeze. Our go-to food places and inviting close friends and relatives every other day of the week. Learning to cook each other's favourite dishes, just like how our mothers used to make them. Visiting different cities, and driving back home together, humming softly into the night. Planting plum trees in our back garden. Adopting stray kittens and giving them ridiculous names. When we disagree, there will be no yelling, but apologies and embraces. This will be our life, and it'll be full of love.

Simple and beautiful.

It's raining where I am. I hold my head upwards
and wonder if it's dry where you are. I picture your palms, reaching out to feel the sun. I like to think you're somewhere in Marrakesh, reading a book and sipping Moroccan mint tea by the hotel pool. I picture you stumbling over the menu, just a little, the foreign language feeling uncertain on your tongue.
During the afternoon you linger by the market, picking out a handmade bracelet
you think I might like.

You must love it there. I always thought the rain was your way of saying you were thinking of me. I hope it's warm where you are. I hope you know
I'm thinking of you too.

Even when they tie the white cloth
around my chin upon death
you will not leave my heart.
You,
my guiding light in the storm of life.
The true north
on my heart's compass.
When the dusts of earth envelop my corpse,
I will still think of you
and long after.

You're so far from me. I imagine the ground folding like a map so I can stride across it. Jump over the horizon to get to you.
In my head we are neighbours.
In my head we wake up side by side.
I picture the land between us connecting like hands in prayer. I picture my arms reaching across the ocean to bring you here. Or I'll come on boat, rowing against the currents until I'm washed up against your doorstep saying *"hello,*
I'm here.
Look how I've travelled
the earth for you."

- Inspired by Azra.T 'the worlds gift'

"What is life without her?" they ask him.
"What is the sea
without its water?"
he replies.

He carves her name into branches.
Eats from the same bowl that she eats
from.
Finds the scent of her in his jackets that
she's borrowed. Discovers that she loves
all the things he loves.

i.

He addresses a letter to her from Nowhere, and she sits by it for hours, cheeks warmed from a heart beating too fast.

She opens it while moonlight goes off, and the storm blows against her roof.

He's sent her a piece of himself, and she wonders about the doors it would knock, if she returned it back to Nowhere.

iii.

He looks up at the night sky. Orion above the horizon and, near it, Jupiter. He wonders if she could see it, too. He wonders if their stars were the same.

But he'll be seeing her soon.

And it will be better than anything else.

"I've missed you for too many winters," he says. "I'm coming back."

iii.

He brought peace in with him,

closed the door on the November wind

and sat with her by the fire.

"Tell me what it's like, in Nowhere," she asks him for the millionth time. He guides her to bed, tucking her in and making sure her feet are covered.

"Lonely without you," he admits. "But I've brought back stories."

He tells her about how the stars change beyond the equator. How there are places where it looks like there are twin suns. How the desert crawls into you but so does snow. He talks about the taste of fruit, like nectar on the tongue. She falls asleep while he murmurs about oceans, about rivers.

- To Nowhere

I imagine us walking along side by side
through an empty street corner
in an ancient city.

We're holding hands,
and your eyes brighten
as you tell me about something you love.

And I'm just happy to witness you.

ANTIOUITES
e grenier

The Losing

In this short life that only lasts an hour
can't you stay here a little longer? I'll turn on the kettle
and pour you another cup of chai. We can talk about the
weather, how things are going, if you're okay?
Please linger near the door uncomfortably
instead of leaving without a goodbye.
Please forget your coat or wallet
and come back later for it
in the night.

- Inspired by Mikko Harvey's 'for m'

In my favourite daydream, I come home to you
and we're laughing over dinner;
we're reading in the rooftop garden
you made out of two half-dead plants
and a picnic table. We stay up curled around each other
quietly discussing the plot to our favourite series.
I can imagine it.
Lazy days with you,
in the good quiet wonder of regular mornings
with laundry and matching socks
and where it's all perfect.

But to my heart I say,
you're better off keeping away,
because in dreams people can't hurt you.
And in dreams people tend to stay.

one.

Tell me about the wedding you'll never have and the life you'll never share together. The children, the home with a picket fence and cat snoozing by the door side. You'll end up with someone else, you will. But still.
Still.
If there is a universe where you're growing old by his side, I just know.
That you're very happy in it.

two.

I know he curves your lips into a smile
and your heart feels safe inside his steady palms.
But you have parted ways
for a reason.
You are a gem of a woman and you will find someone
who makes you feel like the lightest element, brighter
than any sunrise, like a kite running loose in the wind,
you will - but it's just…
not going to be him.

- Message to a friend

Dear love,

I wanted to point out the future and say: See that light? In that brightness we are destined. I just wanted to protect you. No more bad days. Just a good candle and a long, lazy morning. You could have taught me all the magic made in the kitchen. I could have taught you books. Poetry. Taken you to the cabin by the lakeside. Shown you where the rarest bluebells grow. It would have been nobody but us and the gentle rain falling.

Instead you had to be a river I couldn't swim in. A bird I had to learn to let go.

I'm supposed to be better now, I think, but my breath still catches on your ghost sometimes.

Dear reader,

November is here. The month of darkening skies and birds parting. The time of year that feels like that moment in a good book when there's only a few pages left. You don't know how the story will end only that soon you'll have to say goodbye
to something beautiful.

Dear friend,

life right now feels like a fog I'm trying to pass through. I try to laugh when I can but mostly I just miss the world. Simpler times. Early mornings in your car, heading to someplace new or someplace far. Watching the sunset from the top of a hill. Weekdays in the mosque, weekends gathered by the bonfire.
I took a lot for granted this year.
Now I feel those days like something sharp in my heart.
But I'm rambling now. And it's getting late here.
I hope you're doing well.

Dear mum,

I've got the blues again. I'm backsliding into old habits and slower mornings and after all this work and all this time - the window of my heart still overlooks something horrible. I've heard somewhere how negative spaces say so much. I'm frequently worried I am only negative spaces.
Will you cradle me until the sun comes back to dry the ground? Until I'm ready to grow again?

I'm sad, mum,
but I can only write about it.

I leave my eyes open.
I lie here and forget our life
of summers spent together huddled under jasmine trees,
reciting Persian poetry.
of sailing on my grandfather's old wooden boat
into the emptiness of the night
whilst the stars would reflect themselves
onto sea
and you'd point up
naming every constellation for me.

I try not to cry
but I can't.

I try to forget
but it's so hard.

You used to sleep so you could meet him.
It was that simple.
You'd rush towards him in summer twilight. Not in the real world, but in the buried one where he was waiting.
He'd stand far in the distance, arms outstretched.

What have you been doing?
you'd whisper once you reached him,
and he'd smile and take your hand.

Nothing. Just waiting for you.

Waking up from those dreams were always a nightmare recurring.
Each morning you felt the pangs of grief in waves,

a sickness that went on
and on.

I have heard somewhere
that soldiers who lose
an arm or leg
still feel the pain in those limbs,
though they are gone.

It is like that sometimes…

I can feel you with me,
though you are gone,
and it is like I am missing

a part of myself.

Remember how you promised me once
to never leave me?
Yet now, in death,
you have run off to a place
so far away.
A place where I cannot reach you
nor
can I follow you there…

The year of letting go

January

Every time you utter the word 'goodbye',
it goes into me like a knife.
I know they say love is an acceptable form of insanity but
I'm tired of losing my mind for you.
Tired of waiting in the rain for you.
Tired of walking through traffic blindly
wondering if getting hit would hurt less than this.

February

"I wish you had stayed."
I watched you struggle to find the words to reply. You
ran a hand through the length of your face. Sighed. "I
would have poisoned your life."
"You have already poisoned my life." I swallowed the
lump in my throat. "When you left me alone
in it."
You said nothing, and we stood there in the silence,
two small stars,
with the universe expanding
between us.

March

I keep your words tucked away at the back of my mind. I'm humming your name in the grocery store. Can't shake the shape of your smile. I go home and make myself stew.
Tell myself I'm fine alone.

But I know I'll fall asleep missing you.

April

In this story you're sitting on the front porch of my ribcage. You want to leave but my veins wrap around you like ivy. You tear yourself free and all the lights go off. I lay on the floor in the room of my heart after you slam the doors shut. I reach out into the darkness and every vessel I find is cold to the touch. In this story, the lights never come on. In this story,
you never come back.

May

There's a lot of things I would say to you if I were brave enough. They pile up in the base of my throat and I let them sit there. I wish goodbye didn't mean goodbye but *I'm leaving for now not forever* and *wait for me. Someday soon we'll be together again.*

I don't know…it's just that my thoughts seem to revolve around you. Over and over.
I hope you're doing okay.

June

Remember when we kept the windows open and let the snow fall in? We watched it pile up on our floorboard like a Serbian landscape. You let your body slide onto the ground and asked me to join you. Dropped your head on my shoulder and told me you could just die like this. They were the days when I could feel the cold when you shivered, ached when you weren't holding my hand. It didn't matter that we couldn't afford central heating, not when the warmest place was next to you.

I still don't know what love is made out of,
but at the time, I guess…I thought it might have been you.

July

Every poem I have ever written is trying to get closer to the people I have lost, and it's failing.
You're the furthest star in my milky way.
You exist somewhere all these thoughts

can't even touch.

August

I remember once
when you told me
"tell me where it hurts
and I'll make it better"
but where are you now
seven and a half months later
when I'm lost
in such deep sorrow
whispering
"everywhere."

September

It's almost autumn and I'm so glad
because the summer
smelt like you.

October

Last night I had a dream where I dragged your body to safety before the dragon could swallow you. It dragged me into the tower instead.
We ate figs under the shade of your favourite tree.
You leaned forward, your brows pressing against mine
before I evaporated
into nothing.

November

Once we had loved each other.
At least there was that.
I knew your fears and the colour of your favourite
sweater.
And yeah, months have passed since we've spoken
and maybe spiders don't scare you
like they used to.
And maybe that yellow sweater your grandmother made
fell apart because you wore it too much.
But once we had loved each other
and I am content
knowing that.

December

It's a small hope I have, maybe.
We'll both be boarding the same plane someday and
bump into each other by the entrance. Or I'll get a call
from an unknown number a few years down the line, and
it'll be your familiar voice that murmurs, 'hey
you...remember me?'
It's a small hope to tuck beneath my arm that I carry with
me. But it's a hope,
and that's something.

One day
when the curse of time
weakens my memory,
I will sit on my rocking chair
recalling
the softness we exchanged
the moments shared
the pain
as well as the laughter.
I will hold onto them tightly
with my fraying hands

and *I will remember.*

Angels

Last night I heard the angels say your name. I woke up with my ears ringing and fell back asleep to dreams where again you leave. I think I'm getting used to those. Even in my head I'm too tired to scream at you anymore. Even in my head I just stand there and say, "okay, but come back if you can."

There are two people asleep at the tables in the back of the library. I wonder if they're dreaming of those they left behind, or if they're too tired to dream at all.

Today a friend told me she separated with her fiancé of two years. She didn't cry. "Who has time for love?" she said. "I have a degree to ace and essays to write." I wonder if she nightmares now, or if she sleeps easy. I wonder if she sometimes has the urge to call him but swallows down the bite of lonely. Instead relies only on the deep agony of putting yourself first. She needs her education. She's going to be a physiologist. I'm proud of her, and also deeply, terribly sad.

"Sometimes you have to give people up because life makes you choose between your heart and your survival," she tells me a while later, when we're waiting at the bus stop under grey skies. He used to pick her up from campus every evening. Now she stands next to me in the cold, cheeks damp and shivering.

"Being with him was as easy as eating food or drinking water. The problem was never him..." she falters, trying to hold herself together. "It was the road we were travelling that was hard."

Last night I heard the angels sing. I woke up and the first thing I thought of was to tell you what their chorus sounds like. And then I remembered you are on a journey that I'm no longer a part of. Treading a path I don't understand. Though our wings touched for the briefest moment, it was really beautiful,

being part of your life.

The Healing

The way light fades away as the day
comes to an end.
Clings to every last thing it can
just half a second longer.
Then sighs,
and gently lets go.
If we could be more like light:
Hold tightly to what matters
but know when to let go
when we know it's time.

Concept:

I make peace with your absence. The name of you stops gnawing at my throat. My house is always warm. I open the curtains and let the sun back in again. Nights are short and quiet and soft. I can sit in silence without it being deafening.
I can be alone without being lonely.

You weren't made for this world, but you still have to live in it. I'm sorry you're hurting. If I met you I think I'd adore you for the rest of my life. If I met you I would guard you with a love that heals. A balm against the ache. I'd fill your heart with a heaven of stars. Take your sorrows and wield them against my back so you never have to feel the weight of it.

If I could be there on your bad days. Press a warm cup of cocoa into your hands, place a plate of fresh fruit on your nightstand. Sit with you while the waves roll, and let you know you're not alone in this.

I'd tell you something my father told me last summer, while I was helping him water his orchard:

Plants take time to spread their roots before you can even see their first leaves. Which is to say, just because you can't see progress does not mean you aren't making any.

Cry when you need to. There is no shame in feeling, so feel it all. Grief is still grief if no one has died. Loss is loss. Goodbyes are goodbyes. But they will be followed by new hellos and good mornings and embraces. I pray you encounter the softest places. A sweetness. All honey and gold. I hope you sleep and wake up well-rested and you wake up happy and you wake up home again.

But for now, we have to keep going, no matter how many times our skies come falling. Just for now, we'll keep going, and take the sun with us into the colder months.

- A little note, a little love

To long for simple things. The way your cat will give gentle headbutts to show its trust. How your child will wrap their tiny hands around your thumb. Planting your own garden. Decorating your own home. The idea that one day you'll fall into bed beside someone you love… you have to romanticise your future, even on days like this.

I used to long for the winter cold
to push us into each other's arms.
But now everything smells like frost and sadness.

I still think of you too often but I'm getting better
at concealing it.

The snow looks beautiful against the blue of the sky.

I drink spiced chai
and try new things
and visit familiar places.

I thought I would be ruined by you
but look at me,
still standing.

I've learnt how to cook mama's famous roast chicken
and I take grandpa with me on walks
in the mornings.
        I enjoy things on my own again.

I miss you because I miss having a friend.

But I'm slowly learning
how to feel whole again.

I always write about love but
I've seen a life where you can live without it.
Where you can eat alone at a table
and be content in the silence.
Where you make the whole bed and slip into it,
cling to your pillow as if it were a person,
and leave the lights on
for yourself.

I speak to You more often and it feels a lot like healing. I read Your book and it wraps its words tight around my ribs and keeps me warm. It doesn't sting so much when I see glimpses of others walking by, hand in hand. I'm happy that they're happy.

I tell myself one day I'll be able to feel it too. My friends still look at me like I might be the loneliest person in all four corners of the globe. "Are you okay?" they ask me. "More than okay," I answer with a smile. Because I have You, my Lord. So I'm not so completely alone. And I know that to have You is to have
the entirety of this world.

Surviving grief (a list)

1. When they're gone, cities will not fall. Empires will not crumble, temples will not collapse. Your home will not go up in a blazing glory like the sky when Rome fell to ruin. When they're gone, rain will not drench the world for forty days and forty nights. When they're gone, the earth will keep turning, and you will get out of bed in the morning.

2. When you clean your skinned heart and close your fist around the idea of love, it will only sting for a second. Run the wound through cool water. Press a soft hand against it. It's okay.
It's okay. Love leaves when it has to. It rushes out with the air when you open the window on a stale November. It's okay. You know it will arrive again. In a different time. In a different form.

3. Boil almond milk and cinnamon sticks, spoon in honey, and stir. This isn't for your winter-worn throat, but for your burning heart.

4. When it gets too much, speak to God. He'll listen - like He always has.

5. You will find comfort in old friendships.
You will look towards your mother
and see the sun.

6. Angels follow you wherever you go. There are prayers you can cast for protection. God is with you in every breath, every moment. Remember this next time you feel alone in the dark.

7. When you sit and reflect on the world, you will notice that there is so much warmth in it. There are roomfuls of people who will jump to help you if you just ask. And they're all trying, putting away their workload to comfort a friend, booking late-night shifts to save a life, taking the day off to watch over their niece. Cats will mourn past owners and crows will play and baby elephants hold their mother's trunk.
How beautiful.
To exist on a planet that's language is love.

8. Pick up old routines. It's time to call your co-workers back. It's time to check out that new Thai restaurant down the street. Some nights the world might seem a little off-kilter, but that's okay. You keep going.

9. Through hardship to the stars. And here you are

floating amongst them.

It's such a relief
when your soul no longer clings to an unattainable person.
When your heart has come to accept that your fate was only meant
to collide for a brief moment in time.
You finally let go of their hand. And get on...
with your big, wonderful life.

Glossary

Aalam-Al-Arwah - Muslim's believe that prior to being born in this world, all human beings were formerly born in a different realm. The state of human beings at the time of that initial birth is referred to as Aalam-Al-Arwah.

Al-Jannah - Arabic word for 'heaven'.

Dua - Arabic word for supplication.

Dunya - In Islam, dunya refers to the temporal world, the opposite to the hereafter.

Fajr - The dawn prayer.

Hadith - Records of the traditions or sayings of the Prophet Muhammad ﷺ.

Inshallah - Translates from Arabic to 'if God wills it'.

Jaan - A term of endearment within many languages that can mean "life", "loved one", "darling" etc.

Jummah - The Friday prayer.

Rasulullah - Translates from Arabic to 'Messenger of God', often attributed to the Prophet Muhammad ﷺ.

Rooh - Arabic word for the 'spirit' or 'soul'.

Salah - Arabic word for 'prayer'.

Surah Furqan - The 25th chapter of the Qur'an with 77 verses.

Thobe - A traditional garment worn by Muslim men.

ﷺ - Translates from Arabic to 'peace be upon him'. It is a prayer and veneration attached to the names of holy figures in Islam, often used after mentioning the name of Prophet Muhammad ﷺ.

Acknowledgement

My infinite thanks to…

My siblings and support system: Samia, my light of inspiration, my trusted editor. Thank you for all your clever ideas and unconditional support.

Nadia, for serving as cover artist, illustrator and a source of guidance; for throwing my initial ideas in the bin but helping me draw up ones that were tons better. You've brought this book to life in more ways than one, and I'd be so incredibly lost without you.

My Nahat, for being a dreamer and fellow bookworm, for never growing tired of listening to my stories (even when they were terrible), and to Sami, for making all those random martial art noises in the background when I was pulling my hair apart writing. I needed that.

The talented Samiha, for saving the day with her digital artistry and technical support. You've been so understanding and patient throughout the process – truly a gift from God.

My dear friend Ads, for every laugh and word of encouragement. You've been cheering me on since the very beginning.

My sun and moon, Fayza and Mariam, who make me believe anything is possible. One day I'll pluck the stars from the sky and fit it into both of your letterboxes.

To little Abid, Aliya, Amreen and Zara for being more excited about this book than I could ever be;

Mars, for being the most reliable person to turn to, and Hanah, who always goes above and beyond.

Honourable mentions go to: Mehmil, Wafa, Ra'ana and Mamuna.

I couldn't dream of having better friends.

And last but not least, a huge thank you to all of my wonderful followers on social media. You have made this book a reality through your endless support, feedback and praise. You're worth your weight in gold. Each and every one of you.

I hope you know that.

Get in Touch!

Writer: Sai Assari
Email: saiassari1998@gmail.com
Instagram: dawnsfragrance

Illustrator: Nadia Hussain
Email: nadiahussain132@gmail.com

Digital Artist: Samiha Yasmin Chowdhury
Email: samihayasminc@gmail.com
Instagram: samihayasminc